My SCHOOL Is WORSE Than Yours

● ● ●

**Written
and Illustrated
by Tom Toles**

VIKING

VIKING
Published by the Penguin Group
Penguin Putnam Inc., 375 Hudson Street, New York, New York 10014, U.S.A.
Penguin Books Ltd, 27 Wrights Lane, London W8 5TZ, England
Penguin Books Australia Ltd, Ringwood, Victoria, Australia
Penguin Books Canada Ltd, 10 Alcorn Avenue, Toronto, Ontario, Canada M4V 3B2
Penguin Books (N.Z.) Ltd, 182-190 Wairau Road, Auckland 10, New Zealand

Penguin Books Ltd, Registered Offices: Harmondsworth, Middlesex, England

First published in 1997 by Viking, a member of Penguin Putnam Inc.

1 3 5 7 9 10 8 6 4 2

LIBRARY OF CONGRESS CATALOGING-IN-PUBLICATION DATA
Toles, Tom.
My school is worse than yours / written and illustrated by Tom Toles.
p. cm.
Summary: Raven, who attends an underground school with a robot
teacher, pursues her dream of being an artist.
ISBN 0-670-87336-5
[1. Artists—Fiction. 2. Schools—Fiction. 3. Robots—Fiction.]
I. Title.
PZ7.T5742My 1997
[Fic]—dc21 96-36887 CIP AC

Printed in U.S.A.
Set in New Century Schoolbook

For Amanda

Contents

1

The Worst School in the Universe

My grandfather is a hat.

A soft black hat, the kind that flops over on one side of your head.

It hangs in my grandmother's back hall.

My grandmother said my grandfather always wore that hat when he went out.

Then he died. Before I was born.

The hat seems to be all that is left of him—all I've ever seen, anyway, and so, to me, that hat is my grandfather.

My father says that his dad, my grand-father, the hat, can see me from heaven. I wonder if he can see me now.

I'm sitting here in my yellow plastic chair at my yellow plastic desk in the worst school in the universe. My name is Raven. Raven Royce.

I have to tell you about my teacher. You won't believe it. She's a robot. I don't mean she's *like* a robot, she *is* a robot. The only one in this horrible school. Her name is Mrs. Rust.

My dad says they made her a few years ago when they thought that robots would be doing all the jobs. Mrs. Rust was the first robot teacher. She didn't turn out too well. They didn't make any more. But they had spent so much money making her that they had to keep her.

Her official name is Robotic School Teacher, or RST. But everybody calls her Mrs. Rust.

Let me tell you about my day.

Class started the way it always starts,

with a really frightful squeaking noise, like when you scrape the tip of your fork on the dinner plate the wrong way, only louder.

It was Mrs. Rust turning her head to look at the class with her little video-camera eyes. Her head always squeaks like that when it turns. They said I'd get used to it. I haven't.

"Raven, come up to the chalkboard," she said. She doesn't sound much better when she talks. Her mechanical voice isn't too bad, although it's not very friendly sounding, but her jaw joint squeaks too, which makes it hard to hear what she's saying sometimes.

And you can't see what she's saying by watching her lips, because she doesn't have any lips. Not moving ones, anyway, just red strips of plastic above and below her awful teeth, which are really just short pieces of chalk set in little metal sockets.

I guess it makes sense for a teacher to have chalk for teeth—except for when she gets angry and her jaw hinges start working extra hard, banging her mouth open and

shut with such power that the chalk shatters and flies around the classroom. Then she looks really terrible until Mr. Bleek, the assistant principal, comes and replaces the missing and broken teeth with new chalk stubs. Mr. Bleek never says anything.

I put on my boots and headed to the chalkboard.

We need boots in our school because the school leaks quite a bit and there are puddles on the floor. Our classroom crayfish lives in the puddle by the wall, under the plant table that teaches us how vegetation always dies in a classroom setting.

Our school leaks because our school was built completely underground, back when they thought there might be a war and we'd be safer underground. They stored huge cans of crackers here so we could survive for years without coming out. They are still serving those crackers in the cafeteria.

The bombs never came, but the water did.

My regular classroom has puddles, but some others are worse.

The water in my social studies class was once so deep that we had to use a little rubber raft to get around. For a while, there was a big wooden lifeboat hanging on the wall (in front of the poster telling us how special we all are) in case there was a fire and we all had to get out at once. I didn't think that made much sense.

My social studies teacher is Mr. Crevice.

He is not a robot, but he's pretty awful, too. He does weird things—like when the class is acting up, he puts Chapstick all over the lenses of his glasses, so, he says, he won't have to look at us.

And he gives weird assignments. For geography he had us make a salt map of his face, and then label his mouth as a canyon, his nose as a volcano, and his wrinkles as river valleys.

So anyway, I was splashing my way to the chalkboard thinking about my project in art class. I *love* art class.

Raymond Wise turned around and smirked at me because I had to go to the board and he didn't. This I could deal with. As I passed him, I stamped my foot a bit and shot a blob of puddle onto the side of his head.

2
The Math Problem

I knew there was going to be trouble today. There was always trouble when I had to come up to the chalkboard.

"Raven!" squalled the hinge on Mrs. Rust's jaw. "Solve this math problem for the class."

I don't like math problems.

But it was worse this time. There was no problem on the chalkboard, just some mushy streaks. This had happened once before.

Mrs. Rust had a habit of turning her head around backward when she wrote on the chalkboard, so she could keep an eye on the class. When she did this, the kids would all smile at her.

Fake smiles. Like a wall of painted smiling faces. So she'd think they were behaving. Sometimes they were, and sometimes they weren't.

Being a robot, she really didn't need to look where she was writing.

Except sometimes she made a mistake.

Like this time.

Instead of grabbing a piece of chalk, she had grabbed a toadstool that was growing in the damp wooden chalk tray. She had been

writing with that. It didn't write. It just made mushy streaks on the chalkboard.

I was scared.

Mrs. Rust didn't think she could make mistakes. She figured she was a machine, a perfect machine.

When something went wrong, it was somebody else's fault. Somebody nearby. I was nearby.

My fault.

I couldn't move. I couldn't talk.

Finally she turned her head and looked at the board. *Squeak.*

The kids changed their fake smiles into real smiles. They were laughing. At Mrs. Rust. At me.

Mrs. Rust looked back at the class. *Squeak.*

Fake smiles again.

Then she looked at me. *Squeeeeeak.*

I didn't know what to do. Mrs. Rust was waiting for an answer. An answer to a problem that wasn't there.

I could say, "Mrs. Rust, you wrote with a toadstool instead of chalk."

The class would laugh. But Mrs. Rust wouldn't laugh.

I was doomed.

Of course, even if I could see the problem, I probably wouldn't get it right. I can do math okay, but I tend to rush, and I make mistakes. Especially when I'm at the chalkboard standing next to Mrs. Rust.

Sometimes I just guess at the answer. So that's what I decided to do. Guess. I marched over to her mushy streaks, pretended to be thinking, and confidently wrote the number 5.

Mrs. Rust looked at my 5. Then she looked at me. *Squeak.* "Very good, Raven," she said. "Five is correct."

I nearly fainted.

The kids in the class clapped and cheered.

Mrs. Rust swung her head around to look at them. They put their fake smiles back on.

I walked back to my seat in triumph.

Genius. Genius Raven. Can solve problems nobody can see.

I skidded on the slippery floor and almost fell. A couple of kids laughed.

Well, I was a genius for a minute, anyway.

3
Sliding Food

I always walk to lunch with my friend Melody. The hall in our school is pretty dark. And scary.

There's only one lightbulb. It hangs down on a wire. And it's burned out.

And there's water in the hall, like everywhere else in the school. Except the hall is slanted, and the water along the wall of lockers flows in a little stream.

Caspar Thumb, Raymond Wise's best friend, made a paper boat today. He drew a pirate flag on it and put it in the stream. It floated along next to Melody and me as we walked.

"Ugly girl off the starboard bow," Caspar announced. "Prepare to meet your fate."

"Should I punch his lights out?" I asked.

"Just ignore him. He'll get into trouble eventually without any help from us," Melody said.

I like Melody's name. It's like music.

It's better than mine. Raven. A big black bird. Like a crow. My older sister calls me "Raving," like I'm crazy. I hate it when she calls me that. One time I got so mad about it

I threw my clock at her. It missed. It hit the wall. And broke.

She just said, "See? Raving."

Her name is Angelica. Naturally.

It seems like everybody has a better name than me. Except maybe Caspar Thumb.

Some things in my cafeteria are probably like yours. It always smells like a mixture of food floating in pails of soapy water. And it echoes a lot. Really loud. Like half the kids are yelling that their food is still alive and crawling off their plates, and the other half of the kids are laughing at them.

But some things are different. Like the way you get your food. They decided that it would be faster to put the food on the plates before the kids got there and put the plates on long metal slides. You would pick the row of plates that had what you wanted and push a button at the bottom. Then a metal lever would release the plate and your lunch would slide down to you. That was the idea.

But the way it actually works is that the

rows that have popular foods like pizza and hot dogs have so many plates taken by the time you get there that the ones left are really far up the metal slides. So when you push the button and the plate starts down, it picks up so much speed that when it hits the rubber rail at the bottom, the food shoots off the plate and hits the chairs at the nearest table, which nobody sits at, for obvious reasons.

The other choice is usually something like a plate of tuna melts on stale crackers with cucumbers that haven't been made into pickles.

I usually bring my lunch.

I try to sit as far away as possible from Caspar Thumb and Raymond Wise. They're the dopiest kids in the class. They're like babies. Raymond has his sandwich cut into sixteen little squares, with the crusts trimmed away. And he still ends up throwing most of it into the garbage.

Caspar and Raymond should be about two grades back, if you ask me. If you sit near them at lunch, they gross you out. And that's before they even do anything.

As I walked by them today, I could hear Raymond telling about his mentally ill dog who, when you yell at him for something, comes over and throws up on your foot. Caspar laughed so hard at this that peanut butter squirted out his nose.

I found two chairs at the other side of the cafeteria, under the painting of an old man with a beard who looks uncomfortable, like he has a slice of sour lemon in his mouth. As we sat down and scraped our chairs toward the table, I asked Melody, "Do you think we'll be in this awful school forever?"

She pulled a sandwich and two cookies out of her lunch bag. She handed one of the cookies to me.

"Three or four more years, I guess."

"Forever," we said together.

"Maybe we could do something to fix it up," I said.

"We'll be grandparents before this school gets fixed up," she replied.

I took a bite of my baloney sandwich. Too much mayonnaise. My mother puts mayonnaise on everything.

"How many grandparents do you have?" I asked.

"Four," she said, "and a great-grandmother who's ninety-six."

"One of my grandfathers died before I was born," I said. "I think he was an artist. I want to be an artist. Either that or I want to be the first woman to land on Saturn."

"You can't land on Saturn," Melody said. "I think it's just a big ball of gas. Like Mr. Crevice."

"Then maybe I'll just paint a picture of it."

It was time for art class. Raymond walked by with a napkin all smeared with mustard and catsup.

"I finished my art project," he said. "'Road kill,' it's called."

Now I understood why a guy in a painting on a wall in a school cafeteria would have a sour expression on his face.

4

The Contest

The last part of the day on Tuesdays is art class, the only part I like. When we walked in, the whole day changed.

It's one of the bigger rooms. And not dark at all. The art teacher, Mrs. Blythe, ordered extra lights. She told Mr. Bleek, the assistant principal, that artists were like rare flowers, and we wouldn't bloom without lights. She may have exaggerated a bit there, but she got us our lights.

There are big tables and lots of art supplies: cupboards full of paper, paints, markers, pencils, and pastels.

And Mrs. Blythe is really nice. She has good ideas for art projects, and she really likes the one I'm doing now.

I sat in my favorite chair, the one nearest Mrs. Blythe's desk.

"Raven," she said, "I want to talk to you about your art project."

I brought it over from the green cabinet and carefully laid it on the table in front of me. Mrs. Blythe came and stood next to me to look at it. It was a house. But not just any house. Mrs. Blythe had asked us to make up the best house we could think of.

This was way better than art class last year. Last year my art teacher was Mr. Crevice. The same Mr. Crevice I have for social studies this year. Remember? The one who had us make a salt map of his face. Well, his ideas for art projects weren't any better. He always had us making something out of strange materials.

The time he had us make binoculars out of red clay flowerpots didn't work out too well. They didn't make anything look bigger, and the pots were too large for us to see out of both holes at the same time.

So he had us paint them with pictures of what we'd like to look at with them if they worked. The paint flaked off after about a day.

Then came the toilet-paper-tube phase. You know, those cardboard tubes that are left when the toilet paper is gone. Somehow he got boxes and boxes full of them. He said the number of things you could make out of toilet-paper tubes was limited only by your imagination.

The first idea he had for them was binoculars.

They worked better than the flowerpots, but they still didn't make anything look bigger. Melody told him she thought maybe they made things look a *little* bigger, to make him feel better, I think.

We decorated them with fall leaves. So the birds wouldn't notice us when we watched them.

Then we made toilet-paper-tube wind chimes. They looked okay, but they didn't make much sound, even when we blew at them through our toilet-paper-tube clarinets.

This year, the art projects have been lots better.

"Raven," said Mrs. Blythe, "I like the house you're drawing so much that I'd like to enter it in a contest that *Wonderland* magazine is having. If it's okay with you, that is."

"A contest?" I asked.

"Yes," she said. "It's a contest for the best original design of something people use. First prize is $250."

Mrs. Blythe liked my drawing so much she wanted to enter it in a contest!

And a $250 prize! I could use $250. I could buy more model horses for my collection and still have enough left to have more money than my sister Angelica. She saves all her money in a big glass jar. It's full of dollar bills, and some fives and tens, with a ton of coins on the bottom. She likes to show it to me to prove that she's rich and I'm poor. But I bet it's a lot less than $250.

"But we'll have to hurry," said Mrs. Blythe. "The mailing deadline for the contest is tomorrow."

"But my drawing isn't finished yet!" I said.

5
Winga Winga Winga Whump

My design for a house is a pretty good design, I think.

If you were in an airplane looking down at it, it would look like a giant flower.

I named it "Flower House."

The rooms are all round. With lots of windows in the walls. Big windows divided up into smaller panes.

The rooms are arranged in a big circle,

Flower
House

like the petals of a flower. In the middle of the flower is a big outdoor play area with lots and lots of play equipment. The play equipment is all put together to look like a little castle that you can climb on and climb into. And the castle is made out of pieces that you can take apart and build into different shapes, if you want to.

In the stem part of Flower House is a big room with a glass roof, filled with real flowers in a garden, and a pond with fish in it.

It would be full of light, not like my school. I think it would be fun to live in.

My sister Angelica could live somewhere else.

But I had to finish it. I still had to paint the garden and the climbing-castle. I worked fast and almost ruined it when a spot of red paint dropped off my brush onto the roof. But I saved it by making it into a chimney.

I was finished! And just in time. I showed Mrs. Blythe. She said it was wonderful. She told me to put it in the green cabinet, and she would mail it first thing in the morning.

*   *   *

When the bell rang at two-fifteen, I jumped up and walked as fast as I could (we aren't allowed to run) up the stairs and pushed open the red metal door.

It's weird when you get out of our school.

You can't see it, because it's underground, except for a concrete cube where the stairs and elevator come up to the red metal door. The other reason you can't see it when you get out is because it's so bright outside, compared to inside our school. It's like coming out of an afternoon movie.

I wanted to run, but I had to stand still a minute before I could see. I didn't want to walk into the tree, like I did the first day I went to this school.

It's the only tree near the school. It was there before they built the school. They cut down all the others.

It's a big sugar maple. Last year our science teacher, Mrs. Goodremote, had us drill little holes in it in February, hammer in metal spouts, and fill buckets with maple sap.

If you boil maple sap, the water comes out and you get real maple syrup. It takes a long time. Ours boiled and boiled all day. Then all of a sudden it's maple syrup.

Then all of a sudden it's burnt crusty goo on the bottom of the kettle. That's what happened to ours. We forgot to watch it.

Mrs. Goodremote brought some maple syrup from her house so we could taste it on pancakes. It was good, but I like the regular kind of pancake syrup better.

Now I could see, so I started to run.

I ran all the way down to the crossing guard, the one with the fuzzy blond hair and glasses.

"What's the hurry, Raven?" she asked.

"Mrs. Blythe is going to enter my drawing in a magazine contest! The first prize is $250!" I said, a little out of breath.

"It must be a pretty special drawing," the crossing guard said.

Yes! It is! I thought.

She held up her plastic stop sign and let me cross.

Then I started to run again, fast running, with long leaps over sticks and cracks. I ran all the way home—except for by the red house near the corner of Huckleberry Street, when my side hurt, and I walked until it felt better.

I exploded through our front door, dumped my backpack on the floor, and kicked off my sneakers.

"Mom!" I yelled. Then I remembered that Mom wouldn't be home till later.

I started to run upstairs to my bedroom, but before I got there, I ran back down to the kitchen to get a drink of juice, because I was dying of thirst. I had to breathe hard between every few swallows.

Then I ran up to my room. I did a somersault onto my bed, stood up and started bouncing. My mom doesn't like me to bounce on my bed, but my mom wasn't home.

Then I started to sing. "Winga winga winga whump! Winga winga winga whump!" I sang. "When I sing whump, I drop down on my butt," I said aloud.

"Three wingas, one whump. Winga winga winga whump! And I bounce around the edge of the bed. Winga winga winga whump! And if I land near a corner of the bed on a whump, I get one point. Winga winga winga whump! And if I land away from a corner, I lose a point. Winga winga—"

I stopped. There, standing in my doorway, was my sister Angelica.

"Raving," she said.

6

Angelica's Odd Story

"Angelica," I said, bouncing down and sitting on the edge of my bed, "do you ever wonder about Grampa?"

"Who?"

"Grampa," I said. "You know, the hat in Gramma's back hall. I think Gramma once said he was an artist or something. I think I may want to be an artist."

"Sure, I know all about Grampa," Angelica said.

"Tell me," I said.

"It's a really interesting story," she said. "I'll tell you. For a dollar."

I said, "No way."

"Okay," she said, "it's up to you. It's pretty amazing about Grampa, though."

There was another problem about Angelica. Even if I gave her the dollar and she told me about Grampa, I couldn't be sure it was the true story. She was good at making things up. Especially if she could get a dollar to put in her stupid money jar.

She walked away.

I got a piece of cinnamon gum from my Halloween stash, unwrapped it, rolled it up like a snail shell, and put it in my mouth.

I decided to read. I opened the library book that was on my night table. It was called *The Horse in the Cupboard*. I love horses.

The bookmark was a cardboard horse with three legs. It used to have four, but one got folded inside of books so many times it came off.

The story is about a girl named Oprea who got a magic cupboard for her birthday. If you put a toy inside the cupboard, it was supposed to come alive.

I started to read:

Oprea carefully lifted her favorite horse, a white porcelain Arabian, down from the shelf. She slowly placed it on the wooden bottom of the cupboard and, with trembling hands, closed the cupboard door.

She fitted the tiny gold key into the lock and turned it, hearing a gentle click. She ran to her bedroom door to see if anyone was coming. She could hear her mother walking back and forth in the kitchen.

Oprea tiptoed back to the cupboard, wondering if there had been enough time for the magic to work. She touched the key. It was tiny and smooth on her fingers. She turned it. *Click.* She opened the cupboard door.

And there in the cupboard, were stacks of dishes.

*   *   *

I stopped reading and closed the book. Every time Oprea put a horse in the cupboard, it turned into dishes. Her room was full of them. She had just lost her last horse.

I walked over to my dresser drawer. I had seventeen dollars and thirty-four cents. I took out a dollar.

I put the dollar on top of the dresser and picked up my own horses. Mine aren't made of porcelain. They're hard rubbery plastic. But they're very realistic. My favorite is a brown one with a black mane and tail.

I put four of them on the floor, a mother and father and two sisters.

The older sister was complaining.

"I don't want to be sold to the circus," she said.

"I'm sorry," said the mother horse, "but we need the money to buy oats to eat, and we can get a good price for you from the circus ringmaster."

"Why can't you sell my younger sister instead?"

"We love her too much to sell her," the mother replied, "and we really don't have room here for both of you, anyway. You'll have to be sold, and I don't want to hear another word about it."

I stood up and walked over and picked up the dollar.

I carried it to Angelica's room and handed it to her. She unscrewed the metal top of her money jar and dropped it in with a snooty little flourish that made me want to take out my gum and stick it in her hair.

"Okay," I said, "tell me about Grampa."

"Grampa was a famous artist," she began.

"He was?"

"Yes, he was. He lived in France for a number of years. He was famous for the colors he painted with. They were so pure and bright that they looked almost real enough to touch. He loved painting gardens."

I thought, *The house I drew has a garden.*

"But," continued Angelica, "his eyesight started to fail. He was going blind."

This story was beginning to sound familiar to me. It sounded like a book on Angelica's bookshelf called *Monet's Garden,* about an artist who lost most of his eyesight.

"Grampa painted more and more pictures of his garden. When he was completely blind, he painted his most famous picture, called *Flowers.*

"They were absolutely realistic," Angelica went on. "Nobody could figure out how a blind man had painted flowers that looked so real. The painting was put in the best spot in the Louvre, a French museum. Everyone came to look at it."

I had not heard any of this before.

"Then one day, a little boy touched the

40

painting, which was completely forbidden," Angelica said. "It fell apart. It turns out that it looked so real because Grampa had glued real flowers to the canvas.

"Grampa was arrested and put in jail. He escaped and came to the United States, hiding in a freight train in a bag of rotting potatoes. That hat of his was made out of the potato bag."

She was doing it again. Angelica had a special way of driving me crazy. I didn't know whether she was lying or not, and there was no way I could find out right now. And she knew it.

I thought again about putting my gum in her hair. No, I'd wait until I found out for sure that her story was a lie. *Then* I'd put my gum in her hair.

7
The Experiment

It was all a lie.

I figured this out about a week later in school, by looking at the map. Between France and the United States is the Atlantic Ocean, which Grampa could not have crossed in a freight train.

It was probably too late to get my dollar back. Angelica would just tell me I was remembering her story wrong, or something.

I was still looking at the map when water splashed out of the ocean and sprayed my face. I heard Caspar Thumb laughing behind me.

When I turned, I saw him holding a yellow plastic elephant, the kind you fill with water and squeeze and water shoots out of its nose.

It looked like there was going to be trouble in our classroom today.

Squirting water could be trouble in any classroom, but Mrs. Rust and water were a bad combination.

She's electric.

Whenever she rolls into one of the

puddles on the floor, sparks shoot out of her legs. And then she sometimes says or does strange things. She tries hard to avoid puddles.

The day was mostly normal until after lunch. That's when the trouble began.

"Today," began Mrs. Rust, "we will learn about buoyancy."

The kids had not really settled down yet, so not everybody heard her.

"What did she say?" asked Caspar, who sits behind me. *"Boring-cy?* She's already taught us everything about *that."*

I turned around and whispered, "Shhhh." Then I added, "This might not be boring. She has equipment. An experiment."

On her desk were a large glass bowl filled with water, plastic tongs, and a box with a huge lump of clay in it. The clay, at least, looked promising.

"Buoyancy," said Mrs. Rust. "The upward force exerted upon an immersed or floating body by a fluid."

"*Boring-cy,*" repeated Caspar.

I turned around to say *Shhhh* again and saw Caspar bending over filling his yellow plastic elephant from the puddle on the floor.

He looked up at me and said, "You're right. Maybe this won't be boring. I brought some equipment, too. For an experiment."

Mrs. Rust dug a handful of clay out of the lump and asked, "Will clay float?"

Melody raised her hand.

"Yes, Melody?"

"Clay doesn't float," Melody said. "My mother is a potter, and she keeps her clay in a big bucket of water and it always sits on the bottom, under the water."

"Very good, Melodeedee."

Melodeedee? I thought. *Why did Mrs. Rust call Melody "Melodeedee"?*

I turned around and looked at Caspar. He was giggling.

Then I turned back and looked at Mrs. Rust. She had a wet spot on her forehead. Caspar had squirted her.

She placed her ball of clay in the water with the plastic tongs. It sank to the bottom. "But what happens if I shape the clay into a boat?" she asked.

"It will float!" several kids shouted out.

Then I heard a *friss* sound as Caspar squirted more water. It hit Mrs. Rust on the shoulder as she was turning to grab more clay. There was a hissing sound, and a little cloud of steam came out of her neck.

"Very good, Melodeedee," she repeated, "but what happens if I shape the clay into a bo-bo-bo?"

Caspar was laughing out loud now. So was Raymond Wise.

Mrs. Rust was flattening the new piece of clay out on the tabletop with one hand. With the other, she reached into the bowl with the plastic tongs. She grabbed the sunken lump of clay with the tongs and flung it over her shoulder. It stuck on the letter Q above the chalkboard in the script alphabet.

This was not like Mrs. Rust.

"Bo-bo-bo," she said again.

This was not good.

We would all end up in trouble.

Caspar squirted again. Another hit. A few sparks.

Mrs. Rust's head turned all the way around in a circle. Then her neck got long, like a long pipe, as her head went up into the air.

I had not seen this before.

It came back down with a bang.

She reached for another handful of clay, but grabbed the dirt in the flowerpot on her desk instead. She pulled out the whole potful of dirt, still in the perfect shape of the pot, with the whole plant attached.

"Bo-bo-bo," she said, and put the whole plant into the glass bowl. The water ran over the sides. Mrs. Rust looked at the plant in the bowl with the water everywhere. She was getting herself wetter.

More smoke was coming out of her now, and there was a fizzling, crackling noise.

"Not done," she said. "Have to bake a little longer."

She picked up the bowl and plant and carried it over to the place under her desk where you put your legs when you sit down. This, she must have decided, was an oven now.

She put the bowl into this space and let it go.

It crashed on the floor.

Then she turned a knob on the drawer, like she was turning up the heat. She turned and turned until it came off in her hand. Then she started turning another knob. It came off, too.

She carried a handful of wooden knobs back to the place where she had flattened out the piece of clay. She arranged the knobs on the flattened-out piece of clay and said, "The cookies are done, though."

She picked up the clay plate full of cookie knobs. The plate bent. The cookies rolled off onto the floor. Most of the kids were laughing or talking now. Caspar Thumb was nearly doubled over with laughter.

I watched one of the knobs roll across the floor.

It stopped when it hit a shoe.

The shoe of Mr. Bleek, the assistant principal.

8
Disaster

Suddenly everyone else noticed Mr. Bleek standing there, too.

The room got really quiet.

He walked over and switched off Mrs. Rust.

I don't know how much he had seen, but he walked right over to Caspar, grabbed him by the arm, and marched him out of the room. The yellow plastic elephant dropped to the floor.

The room was *very* quiet.

Mrs. Rust was turned off.

We had never seen her turned off before.

We waited for somebody to come and tell us what to do.

Nobody came.

At one o'clock, some kids started to get up. This was Tuesday, art class day.

I guess they decided we should go to art class, even if nobody told us we could. That was fine with me.

Melody and I walked down the dark hallway as usual. But I had a bad feeling about what had happened in Mrs. Rust's class. I think Melody did, too. She wasn't talking.

Everything seemed bad, somehow.

"I wish somebody would change that lightbulb" was all I could think of to say as we passed the burned-out light hanging down from the ceiling.

"There's a stepladder right there leaning against the wall. How hard could it be to fix it?" It was beginning to seem like the lightbulb stood for everything that was wrong with my school.

We walked into art class. My mood brightened.

Then it darkened.

Mrs. Blythe wasn't there.

At her desk, reading through some papers, sat Mr. Crevice, *last* year's art teacher.

Everything *was* bad.

"Good morning," Mr. Crevice said. "I'll be your art teacher for a few weeks. Mrs. Blythe is ill. She'll be out about a month."

A month! I thought, as I buried my head in my arms.

Then a horrible thought occurred to me. I raised my hand.

"Did she mail my drawing to the magazine contest? Last week was the deadline," I said.

"Magazine contest?" Mr. Crevice asked. "I haven't heard anything about a contest."

I got up and ran over to the green cabinet, where I kept my drawing.

Please be gone! I said to myself. *Please be mailed!*

But there it was.

Unmailed.

Too late now for the magazine contest.

My eyes filled up with warm tears.

I heard a *patt* sound as a drop landed on my picture, right on the red chimney.

9

My Grandfather's Hat

The next weekend, I was at my Gramma's house.

Her house is different from ours. Everything seems to be in exactly the right place. Finished. The tabletops are all neatly arranged and the windowsills have things like colored glass birds on them.

I was still feeling bad about school, and my drawing not getting mailed to the magazine contest. And I was having trouble thinking of fun things to do. That's why I came over to Gramma's house. Sometimes she'll play cards or bake something with me.

But today she was hanging white curtains on the window in her living room. So I hadn't found anything to do here yet, either.

I was sitting in the blue chair with the white and pink flowers. My finger was following the green stems from flower to flower. They didn't all connect. Sometimes my finger had to jump.

Another thing about Gramma's house is there are no toys on the floor. Only a tree in a brown pot and a basket of magazines.

I wandered down to the back hall. There was Grampa's hat. I took it down from the hook, and went back to Gramma.

"Did Grampa get arrested for gluing real flowers on a picture?" I asked.

Gramma laughed. "Not that I remember," she said, "and I think I would remember *that*."

I told her the story that Angelica had told me about him.

She laughed some more.

"No, it wasn't just like that. A train ride across the Atlantic Ocean. No, I don't think so," she said. "But he *was* an artist, you know. And he did love to plan gardens." She tied the curtain back at the side and smoothed it. "And he would have loved you."

"He would?" I asked.

"Oh, yes, Raven. You're creative in the same sort of way he was."

"I like his hat." I had put it on and was standing in front of a mirror. It actually looked kind of good on me.

"That was his favorite hat," Gramma said. Then she looked at me as though she was thinking. "You can have it if you like."

I didn't say anything right away.

Then I told Gramma about how my drawing never got sent in for the contest, because Mrs. Blythe got sick.

"Well, I'd love to see it," Gramma said. "It reminds me of something that happened to your grampa.

"When he was just starting out as an

artist, he entered a painting in an art show. He was very much hoping to win a prize. He didn't. So naturally he felt that he had failed. That he never could be an artist."

"He did?" I asked.

"Oh, yes. But the day before the show ended, the editor of a magazine came to look at the paintings. He liked Grampa's painting so much that he asked your grampa if he could put it in his magazine. Grampa said yes, and it ran in the very next issue, right on the cover."

"What happened then?" I asked.

"After that, he did a lot more work for magazines. So sometimes things work out well, but in a different way than you expect."

"Gramma," I said.

"Yes, Raven?"

"I think I would like Grampa's hat."

10
The Accident

I started wearing my grandfather's hat to school.

At first I was afraid that somebody would laugh. But Gramma had told me that Grampa *never* worried that people would laugh at him. After that first art show, if he liked something, he stopped worrying about who else liked it.

He was self-confident. I wanted to be like

that. So I wore the hat. Nobody laughed. Melody said it was the coolest hat she'd ever seen.

When I got to school, I folded it carefully and put it in my knapsack.

In my knapsack was the lightbulb I had brought to school. I decided I was going to fix the bulb in the hall if it killed me.

And as it turned out, it almost did.

The day started out pretty normal, at least, normal for our school.

Mrs. Rust was fixed, except now she always wore a rubber raincoat so she wouldn't get wet and start baking things in her desk.

Caspar Thumb had been pretty quiet since he was told he would have to mop the puddles off the floor every day.

Parents were starting to say someone was going to have to solve the water problem in the school.

Mrs. Rust finished her experiment on buoyancy. She made a clay boat and it floated. That proved the principle of buoyancy, but I'm still not sure what the principle is.

But on the way to art class that day, something happened that I'll never forget for the rest of my life.

I stopped by the hanging bulb in the hall. I was carrying the new bulb I had brought to fix the light with. I set it down on my books in a dry spot in the hall and brought over the ladder that was leaning against the wall. I put it under the bulb and climbed up five steps. I remember Melody said, "Hurry up."

I reached up to unscrew the old bulb. This part I don't remember too well. When I touched the metal socket above the bulb, suddenly I felt a funny tingling in my hand,

like wiggling worms. I pulled my hand away so fast I lost my balance. The ladder tipped and I started to fall. Melody said something I didn't hear. Then everything went black.

I didn't know where I was.

It was dark, like the hallway, except for a bright light above me. Had I changed the bulb? I wondered.

No, because out of the light came a face. A man. He was looking at me. Somehow I knew who it was.

"Grampa?" I said.

"Yes, Raven," he said.

I was a little confused. A lot confused. "You're dead," I said.

"Yes, that's true," he answered.

"Does that mean I'm dead?" I asked.

"Well, you're not in very good shape just now," he said. "You hit your head when you fell off the ladder."

Then he just looked at me awhile. It was nice. Peaceful.

Then he said, "But it's not your time to die

now. It's time for you to wake up."

Then the light around him started to grow dim.

"Grampa," I said, "I love you."

"I love you, too, Raven. I always have. You have good taste in hats."

"Thanks," I said. But even then it seemed like kind of a dumb thing for me to say.

Grampa was fading away, going back to wherever he had come from.

And just before he disappeared, he said, "You might want to change the name on your drawing from 'Flower House' to 'Flower School.'"

11
Famous

When I woke up, it seemed everyone in the school was crowded around me.

"Raven," the school nurse was saying. "Can you hear me?"

Then they lifted me onto a stretcher that they wheeled into an ambulance. There were a lot of people outside the school, too. Then the ambulance door closed and I heard the siren as they took me to the hospital.

*　*　*

It turned out I was fine.

I was only there one day, but a lot of people came to visit me. Even the crossing guard with the fuzzy blond hair and glasses. Melody brought me a horse for my collection. A porcelain one!

My mom and dad brought me a book. It's the sequel to *The Horse in the Cupboard*. It's called *The Horse in the Refrigerator*. I can hardly wait.

My sister Angelica came in and stood next to the bed for a minute, then reached into her pocket and handed me a dollar. When she turned, I noticed a funny notch cut out of the back of her hair.

"What happened to your hair?" I asked.

"Nothing," she answered. "When you weren't home, I started reading your stupid horse book. I sat down on your bed, and when I leaned back, my hair touched the headboard of your bed, right where you left an old piece of gum."

"Gee, Angelica" was all I could think of to

say, "what a place for me to leave my gum!"

My last visitor was Mrs. Blythe, my art teacher, who had been in the same hospital and had left only one day before. She was better now.

"I'm so sorry I wasn't able to mail your drawing of the house to the magazine. I got sick so unexpectedly," she said.

"That's okay," I replied.

Then I remembered, or thought I remembered, what my grandfather said.

"But it's not a picture of a house," I said to Mrs. Blythe. "It's a school."

Mrs. Blythe stopped and looked out the window for a minute.

"That's odd you should say that, Raven," she said, "because just today I was put on a committee to come up with a design for a new school building to replace the awful one we're in now. And as I think about it, your design would be *perfect* for a school."

Well, I got my picture in the newspaper twice that month. Once for being taken to

the hospital from our old school, and once for coming up with the design for our new school.

In the second picture with me were Mrs. Rust, in her rubber raincoat, and Mr. Crevice, and—most important—Mrs. Blythe.

I was smiling my proudest smile, and there on top of my head was my grandfather's hat.

Tom Toles is a Pulitzer Prize–winning editorial cartoonist whose work is seen in more than two hundred newspapers and magazines in the United States and Canada. He has also won the H. L. Mencken Free Press Award, the John Fischetti Prize for Editorial Cartooning, and the Global Media Award for environmental cartooning. Five collections of his editorial cartoons and one of his comic strip, "Curious Avenue," have been published.

Tom Toles says that he wrote *My School Is Worse Than Yours*, his first children's book, because there was a certain hat that needed a story. He and his wife, Gretchen, and two children live in Hamburg, New York.